DARK SIDE
POCKET EXPERT

Written by Catherine Saunders

CONTENTS

HOW TO USE THIS BOOK

This book is organized alphabetically, so use the contents list above to find the character or location you're looking for. Difficult words or terms are explained in the glossary on p. 78, and below is a key to the abbreviations used for each character's appearances in the Key Facts box.

C: Star Wars comics
N: Star Wars novels
THR: The High Republic
I: Star Wars: Episode I The Phantom Menace
II: Star Wars: Episode II Attack of the Clones
CW: Star Wars: The Clone Wars animated
TV series
BB: Star Wars: The Bad Batch animated
TV series
III: Star Wars: Episode III Revenge of
the Sith
TJ: Star Wars: Tales of the Jedi animated
TV series

JFO: Star Wars: Jedi: Fallen Order
video game
S: Solo: A Star Wars Story
OWK: Obi-Wan Kenobi TV series
R: Star Wars Rebels animated TV series
RO: Rogue One: A Star Wars Story
IV: Star Wars: Episode IV A New Hope
V: Star Wars: Episode V The Empire
Strikes Back
VI: Star Wars: Episode VI Return of the Jedi
M: Star Wars: The Mandalorian TV series
VII: Star Wars: Episode VII
The Force Awakens
VIII: Star Wars: Episode VIII The Last Jedi
IX: Star Wars: Episode IX The Rise
of Skywalker

Darth
Vader

3

WHAT IS THE DARK SIDE?

To understand the dark side, first you need to know about the Force. The Force is an invisible energy that surrounds all living things. It has a light side and a dark side. Some individuals have the ability to use the Force; it can give them great power.

Those who follow the light side, such as the Jedi, help others and strive for peace, but those who follow the dark side, such as the Sith, spread fear and seek power.

THE SITH

The Sith Order was created by frustrated Jedi who felt that the Jedi were wasting their abilities. The resulting wars between the Jedi and Sith eventually left only one Sith alive: Darth Bane.

In this book you will meet some of the worst folk in the galaxy. Driven by greed, hate, and revenge, they have chosen the dark side. Some started out as Jedi, while others come from generations of dark side users. Many of the most feared dark side users are Sith, members of an ancient and secretive order. The dark side gives the Sith amazing abilities, but they use them to help only themselves. One thing you can be sure of, those who use the dark side cannot be trusted.

RULE OF TWO

The Sith can't even trust each other, so Darth Bane created the "Rule of Two." This means that there should only ever be two Sith: a master and an apprentice.

AHCH-TO CAVE

The Jedi Order was founded on Ahch-To. This mysterious planet contains many Jedi artifacts that need to be kept safe, so it doesn't appear on any maps. When Rey begins her Jedi training on Ahch-To, the dark side draws her to a mirrored cave.

DARK SIDE CAVE

Rey is desperate to see her parents again and the dark side leads her to a cave of mirrors. However, all she sees is herself. Feeling lonelier than ever, Rey shares her feelings with someone who understands—Kylo Ren.

SITH FACT

Rey's Jedi teacher, Luke Skywalker, worries that she feels drawn to the dark side cave. He also does not trust Rey's bond with his nephew.

AP'LEK

Like all the Knights of Ren, Ap'lek has natural Force abilities and favors the dark side. He is a clever fighter, using tricks and dodges, as well as his mighty ax, to defeat his opponents.

DARK SIDE STATUS

- Fallen Jedi ☐
- Inquisitor ☐
- Acolyte ☐
- Dark Lord ☐
- Other ☑

SITH FACT

Ap'lek's terrifying helmet bears the scars of his many battles. It's been repaired many times, using metal from other armor.

Ap'lek wields a Mandalorian ax

KEY FACTS

Homeworld: Unknown
Species: Humanoid
Height: 1.74 m (5 ft 9 in)
Trained by: Untrained
Appearances: VII, IX, C

MIGHTY KNIGHT

Ap'lek's ax is made from beskar alloy and can slice through armor and bone. He also carries a smoke canister on his waist, which he uses to confuse his enemies.

ASAJJ VENTRESS

DARK SIDE STATUS

- ☑ Fallen Jedi
- ☐ Inquisitor
- ☐ Acolyte
- ☐ Dark Lord
- ☐ Other

Ventress is a former Jedi Padawan turned assassin and bounty hunter. She is strong, cunning, and driven by anger. Wielding two lightsabers, she is a dangerous and agile fighter. Enemies should beware!

SITH FACT

Ventress was born into the Force-sensitive Nightsisters clan, but sold to pirates as a child. She was enslaved until the Jedi Ky Narec found her.

Lightsabers can be joined together to form an S-shaped hilt

KEY FACTS

Homeworld: Dathomir
Species: Zabrak (Dathomirian)
Height: 1.78 m (5 ft 10 in)
Trained by: Ky Narec, Dooku
Appearances: CW, N

8

CHANGING SIDES

Ventress' path to the dark side begins when her Jedi Master Ky Narec is killed. She gives in to rage and revenge. Dooku senses her dark side abilities and recruits her as an assassin. Ventress hopes he will make her his apprentice.

FORMIDABLE FOE

Ventress shows her skills during the Clone Wars. She is more than a match for the Jedi Anakin Skywalker and Obi-Wan Kenobi. However, Dooku and Darth Sidious begin to fear the strength of her Force abilities.

GOING HOME

Dooku orders Ventress' termination, but she survives and returns home to Dathomir. There, Ventress and Mother Talzin plot revenge on Dooku. She also begins a new career as a bounty hunter.

ASHAS REE

SITH FACT

The Sith relic is guarded by traps, but that doesn't stop people from seeking it out. Some wish to use its power, while others want to prevent it from falling into the wrong hands.

A forest planet located in the Outer Rim, Ashas Ree has ancient links to the dark side. It was the site of a Sith temple containing a powerful relic. The Jedi built their own temple on top of the Sith one to seal the relic away. However, the Jedi temple has become a neglected ruin.

FINDING THE RELIC

A traveler named Mika Grey wants to get to the relic before the First Order. However, she triggers a trap and has to be rescued by the crew of a supply ship. Later, Grey activates the relic against the First Order and drains its power.

Ashas Ree has so many forests that it appears green from space

CARDO

Like most of the Knights of Ren, Cardo's origins are a mystery. Although he has dark side abilities, he relies more on his custom-made weapons in battle.

DARK SIDE STATUS

Fallen Jedi ☐
Inquisitor ☐
Acolyte ☐
Dark Lord ☐
Other ☑

KEY FACTS

Homeworld: Unknown
Species: Humanoid
Height: 1.75 m (5 ft 9 in)
Trained by: Untrained
Appearances: VII, IX, C

Cardo's favorite weapon is an arm cannon

SITH FACT

Cardo's custom-built arm cannon contains three weapons: a blaster, a plasma bolt launcher, and a flamethrower.

USEFUL SKILLS

Cardo is a skilled weapons maker and spends hours modifying his weapons. He often works closely with the Knight's Symeong armorer, Albrekh (right).

CAVE OF EVIL

Dagobah is a remote, swampy planet in the Outer Rim. It has a strong connection to the Force, making it an ideal place for Grand Master Yoda to stay safe during the Great Jedi Purge. However, in the Cave of Evil the power of the dark side is strong, giving anyone who enters disturbing visions.

JEDI TRIALS

As part of Luke Skywalker's Jedi training, he must enter the cave. Luke fights a vision of Darth Vader, but behind the Sith Lord's mask he sees his own face. It is a warning that Luke must beware of the dark side.

SITH FACT

When Kylo Ren visits the cave, he has visions of his family. Unable to destroy the image of his parents, Kylo destroys the ancient cave instead.

DARTH BANE

A thousand years before the Clone Wars, the Sith were nearly wiped out in a Jedi-Sith war. Only one survived: Darth Bane. He realized that Sith will always want to destroy each other, so he created the Rule of Two.

DARK SIDE STATUS

- Fallen Jedi ☐
- Inquisitor ☐
- Acolyte ☐
- Dark Lord ☑
- Other ☐

SITH FACT

Bane believed that the Rule of Two would allow the Sith to survive and plot the complete destruction of the Jedi Order in secret.

KEY FACTS

Homeworld:	Moraband
Species:	Human
Height:	Unknown
Trained by:	Unknown
Appearances:	CW

Sith apparition

YODA'S VISION

During the Clone Wars, Yoda travels to Bane's home planet, Moraband. A fiery vision of the Sith Lord tries to persuade Yoda to join the dark side, but he refuses.

DARTH CALDOTH

DARK SIDE STATUS

- ☐ Fallen Jedi
- ☐ Inquisitor
- ☐ Acolyte
- ☑ Dark Lord
- ☐ Other

Very little is known about the ancient Sith Darth Caldoth. His quest for greater Force abilities is thought to have led him into conflict with the Nightsisters and the Jedi, where he proved to be a merciless and cunning foe.

SITH FACT

When Darth Caldoth feared that his Sith apprentice was growing too powerful, he turned him to stone.

KEY FACTS

Homeworld: Duro
Species: Duros
Height: Unknown
Trained by: Unknown
Appearances: N

Flowing black cloak

THE BESTIARY OF DARTH CALDOTH

Darth Caldoth wrote a book about Sith warbeasts. Years later, when young Jedi Dooku found this book in the Jedi Archives, it gave him a troubling vision.

DARTH MOMIN

Unlike many Sith, Darth Momin preferred to create rather than to destroy. However, he believed only in the power of pain and fear, so everything he created was designed to arouse these emotions.

DARK SIDE STATUS

Fallen Jedi ☐
Inquisitor ☐
Acolyte ☐
Dark Lord ☑
Other ☐

SITH TRAINING

Momin's gruesome childhood experiments horrified most people, but the Sith Lady Shaa saw his potential. She made him her apprentice, and trained him until he killed her in a duel.

KEY FACTS

Homeworld: Unknown
Species: Unknown
Height: Unknown
Trained by: Darth Shaa
Appearances: C

Momin used his lightsaber to sculpt this mask

Momin wore the mask at all times

SITH FACT

When Momin died while creating a terrifying superweapon, his consciousness lived on inside his mask.

DARK SIDE STATUS

- [ ] Fallen Jedi
- [ ] Inquisitor
- [ ] Acolyte
- [x] Dark Lord
- [ ] Other

JEDI HATER

Maul has superb combat skills. He is ruthless, agile, and can fight two opponents at once with his double-bladed lightsaber. Trained by Sidious to hate the Jedi, Maul kills Master Qui-Gon on Naboo.

TRUE FAMILY

Maul was born a Nightbrother, but Darth Sidious took him from his family as a child. When Sidious leaves Maul for dead on Naboo, Mother Talzin sends Maul's brothe Savage Opress, to find him. Maul vows to destroy those who have wronged him, including Sidious.

CRIME LORD

Maul wants power as well as revenge. He survives the Clone Wars, Order 66, and even being imprisoned by his former Sith Master. Now, as head of the Crimson Dawn crime syndicate, he is one of the most powerful beings in the galaxy.

DARTH MAUL

Maul was born with a strong connection to the dark side, and always struggled to control his anger. Darth Sidious saw that he would make an ideal apprentice, and spent many years training him to be a fearsome Sith warrior.

Zabraks have two hearts, which give them extra speed and stamina

Most male Zabraks have cranial horns

KEY FACTS

Homeworld: Dathomir
Species: Zabrak (Dathomirian)
Height: 1.83 m (6 ft)
Trained by: Darth Sidious
Appearances: I, CW, S, R

ARE DARK SIDE ABILITIES STRONGER?

All Force users have a range of amazing abilities, such as agility, sensing others' feelings, and moving objects with their minds (telekinesis). However, there are some Force abilities that only dark side followers dare to use. Dark side abilities are not necessarily stronger, but they are driven by negative feelings and designed to overcome opponents quickly.

LIGHTNING

Dark side users can release electricity, also known as Sith lightning, from their hands to cause pain and suffering to their opponents. It can cause disfigurement or death.

CHOKE

Darth Vader has mastered this ability to choke or strangle others without even touching them. He uses it not only on enemies but also on those who fail him in some way.

TRANSFERENCE

Darth Sidious uses the Force to transfer his consciousness from his dying body into a clone form. Later, he wants to use this ability to take over his granddaughter Rey's body.

CLOUDING

Darth Sidious uses the Force to make everyone believe he is simply a helpful politician. He is even able to fool the Jedi.

VISIONS

Both Jedi and Sith can have visions of possible futures. While the Jedi use the light side to remain calm and focused, the Sith are more likely to become troubled and act on them.

POWER OVER DEATH

The ultimate power for many Sith is power over death, and they will do whatever they can to acquire it. Darth Vader is desperate to be reunited with his dead wife Padmé.

POWERFUL BOND

The Force can connect users from across the galaxy, but dark side users can exploit this power to secretly manipulate others. Sidious and Tyranus tried to create a bond with Yoda, but he was able to resist.

SITH FACT

Kylo Ren has a unique Force connection with Rey. They can communicate from great distances and even heal each other using the Force.

DARTH NOCTYSS

DARK SIDE STATUS

- [ ] Fallen Jedi
- [ ] Inquisitor
- [ ] Acolyte
- [x] Dark Lord
- [ ] Other

Like many Sith, Darth Noctyss wants to live forever, and she will stop at nothing to gain power over death. From destroying worlds to controlling others, she does not care what she has to do to achieve immortality.

SITH FACT

Darth Noctyss travels to Exegol, believing that there she has the best chance of learning the secret to eternal life.

Distinctive curved lightsaber blade

KEY FACTS

Homeworld:	Unknown
Species:	Unknown
Height:	Unknown
Trained by:	Unknown
Appearances:	N

A HIGH PRICE

On Exegol, Darth Noctyss takes a new apprentice and performs a ritual to gain immortality. Too late, she learns that her apprentice is Darth Sanguis, a Sith who also tried to achieve immortality and suffered the consequences.

DARTH SHAA

Very little is known about Darth Shaa. Like many later Sith, she conceals her face behind a mask. She favors a two-handed lightsaber fighting style, which can be effective at times, but is no match for her apprentice, Darth Momin.

DARK SIDE STATUS

Fallen Jedi ☐
Inquisitor ☐
Acolyte ☐
Dark Lord ☑
Other ☐

DARTH VS. DARTH

Although she precedes Darth Bane and his "Rule of Two," Darth Shaa follows a well-established Sith tradition of dying at the hands of her apprentice.

SITH FACT

Darth Momin claims that he was never officially Shaa's apprentice, although he admits that he was trained by her.

No one knows why Shaa wears a mask

KEY FACTS

Homeworld: Unknown
Species: Humanoid
Height: Unknown
Trained by: Unknown
Appearances: C

21

CHARACTER

⊛ DARK SIDE STATUS

- ☐ Fallen Jedi
- ☐ Inquisitor
- ☐ Acolyte
- ☑ Dark Lord
- ☐ Other

SITH FACT

Sidious was taught by the mysterious Darth Plagueis. When his training was complete, Sidious killed his master and took on his own apprentice.

PATIENT PLAN

Born Sheev Palpatine to a noble family, Sidious was a senator for his home planet of Naboo. As a politician he is able to subtly manipulate others in order to further his secret plot—to destroy the Jedi and seize power for the Sith.

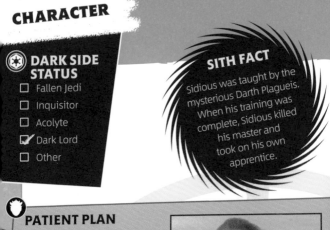

EVIL EMPEROR

When Order 66 is activated, Sidious' plan is complete. The Jedi are virtually eliminated, so no one can stop him from taking control. For many years he rules the galaxy through terror and violence.

⊗ DETERMINED TO RULE

Even Darth Vader cannot stop Sidious. Sith cultists help him to secretly cheat death as a clone on

Exegol. Sidious plots to take his granddaughter Rey's Force abilities to gain the strength he needs to rule again.

DARTH SIDIOUS

Sidious' dark side abilities are so strong that for years he is able to make everyone believe he is just a humble politician. By the time he reveals his true Sith nature it is too late to stop him from taking control of the galaxy.

Face scarred by his own Force lightning during duel with Jedi Mace Windu

KEY FACTS

Homeworld: Naboo
Species: Human
Height: 1.78 m (5 ft 10 in)
Trained by: Darth Plagueis
Appearances: I, II, CW, III, OWK, R, V, VI, IX

DARTH TYRANUS

DARK SIDE STATUS

- ☐ Fallen Jedi
- ☐ Inquisitor
- ☐ Acolyte
- ☑ Dark Lord
- ☐ Other

Darth Tyranus doesn't like rules. He prefers to do things his own way and will use any means necessary to get what he wants. He believes that a Sith Empire will bring order to the galaxy.

Tyranus wears a fancy cloak

KEY FACTS

Homeworld: Serenno
Species: Human
Height: 1.93 m (6 ft 4 in)
Trained by: Yoda, Darth Sidious
Appearances: II, CW, III, TJ

SITH FACT

As the Jedi Master Count Dooku, Tyranus was frustrated and unhappy. He left the Order and later found a new calling as a Sith.

⊗ FORMER MASTER

Tyranus is an agile and cunning opponent, but he also knows when to retreat. Unable to defeat his former Master, Yoda, with the Force or his lightsaber, he distracts him and withdraws.

DATHOMIR

The dark side of the Force is strong on Dathomir. The planet appears red due to the light from its main star, and it is home to many dark side users, including the Nightsisters and the Nightbrothers.

SITH FACT

A powerful green mist, known as spirit ichor, is found on Dathomir. The Nightsisters are able to use it to create magical objects.

ANCIENT RITUAL

Jedi rebel Ezra Bridger and Maul both want to destroy the Sith. They travel to Dathomir to perform an ancient dark side ritual to find out how, but Maul is secretly plotting to make Ezra his apprentice.

DARK SIDE STATUS

- ☐ Fallen Jedi
- ☐ Inquisitor
- ☐ Acolyte
- ☑ Dark Lord
- ☐ Other

SITH FACT

Anakin was drawn to the dark side after troubling Force visions. He wanted the power to save those he loved, including his wife, Padmé Amidala.

Helmet contains breathing apparatus

Armor protects Vader's scarred body

KEY FACTS

Homeworld: Tatooine
Species: Human
Height: 2.02 m (6 ft 8 in)
Trained by: Obi-Wan Kenobi, Darth Sidious
Appearances: III, R, JFO, OWK, RO, IV, V, VI, C, N

DARTH VADER

As a Jedi, Anakin Skywalker was the "Chosen One" who was destined to bring balance to the Force. Arrogance, fear, and frustration led him to the dark side. Now, as Darth Vader, he is the Emperor's terrifying Sith apprentice, feared throughout the galaxy.

FRIEND TO FOE

A duel with former Master and friend Obi-Wan Kenobi on Mustafar leaves Vader close to death. Now, a special helmet and armor keep him alive. They also make him appear even more terrifying.

FEARED ENFORCER

After adopting his suit, Darth Vader fully embraces the dark side. He is ruthless, determined, and shows no mercy to enemies. Even his own officers are terrified of displeasing him.

FAMILY BOND

When Luke Skywalker learns that the feared Darth Vader is his father, he is horrified. Vader, on the other hand is pleased. He wants his son to join the dark side so they can rule the galaxy together.

DRENGIR

They might look a bit like plants, but the Drengir are ferocious carnivores. These bloodthirsty and destructive creatures have a strong connection to the dark side. They share a collective mind, which is capable of corrupting even a Jedi.

JEDI VS. JEDI

The Drengir like to capture their prey and play with them. Here, the Drengir have taken over the Jedi Sskeer's mind so that he will help the Drengir harvest other Jedi.

SITH FACT

Drengir are hard to defeat. Even if they are sliced in half with a lightsaber, one Drengir will just become two!

28

EIGHTH BROTHER

As an Inquisitor, Eighth Brother's only goal is to serve the Empire. He enjoys his work, making sure that he instills maximum fear into his opponents. Impulsive and confident, Eighth Brother is often the first to charge into battle.

DARK SIDE STATUS

- Fallen Jedi ☐
- Inquisitor ☑
- Acolyte ☐
- Dark Lord ☐
- Other ☐

Double-bladed spinning lightsaber can also become a saw-like weapon

KEY FACTS

Homeworld: Terrelia
Species: Terrelian Jango Jumper
Height: Unknown
Trained by: Darth Sidious, Darth Vader
Appearances: R

SITH FACT

Eighth Brother does not rely on his dark side skills alone; he also carries small explosives to throw at opponents.

Tall, agile build is typical of his species

DOWNFALL

Eighth Brother's impulsive nature is his undoing in a battle against Maul and the Jedi. Outnumbered and with a damaged lightsaber, he cannot win.

EXEGOL

Dark, rocky, and prone to lightning, Exegol suits the Sith Order well. Situated in the Unknown Regions, it is the perfect place for Darth Sidious to hide when everyone believes him to be dead. This is where he secretly plots to take over the galaxy once again.

SITH FACT

Before the Sith came to Exegol it was a green and fertile planet able to support many forms of animal and plant life.

Dust particles create a dark atmosphere even inside the Citadel

BARELY ALIVE

Darth Vader thought that he had killed Sidious, but his master had prepared for death and transferred his mind

to a cloned body on Exegol. He is kept alive by the power of the dark side and the loyal Sith Eternal cultists.

FINAL ORDER

The final part of Sidious'
plan is an enormous fleet
of Star Destroyers, known
as the Final Order. Each
ship has the power to
destroy whole planets.
If they are unleashed, the
Resistance will have little
chance against them.

SITH TROOPERS

Sidious has spent many years
preparing to regain his position
as ruler of the galaxy. He has
created an army of loyal
red-armored troopers on
Exegol, ready to do whatever
he asks of them.

Rey finds
her way to
Exegol
and faces
Sidious

Sidious'
Sith
lightning

FIFTH BROTHER

DARK SIDE STATUS

- ☐ Fallen Jedi
- ☑ Inquisitor
- ☐ Acolyte
- ☐ Dark Lord
- ☐ Other

No one is exactly sure how and when this former Jedi turned to the dark side. However, it would be hard to find a more ruthless and committed Jedi hunter than Fifth Brother. His ambition is to be the next Grand Inquisitor.

Fifth Brother takes his mission very seriously

SITH FACT

Despite his position, Fifth Brother is not highly skilled with a lightsaber. Instead he relies on his Force abilities, such as telekinesis and reading others' minds.

KEY FACTS

Homeworld: Unknown
Species: Unknown
Height: Unknown
Trained by: Darth Sidious, Darth Vader
Appearances: C, OWK, R

GETTING IN THE WAY

During the hunt for the Jedi Obi-Wan Kenobi, Fifth Brother has the backing of Darth Vader and a battalion of stormtroopers. However, he is still outsmarted by Third Sister's clever tactics.

FORTRESS INQUISITORIUS

Located mostly underwater, the Inquisitors' headquarters is ominous, menacing, and heavily armed. It is located on the water moon, Nur, hidden far away in the Outer Rim. Few would dare visit Fortress Inquisitorius, even if they were able to find it.

SITH FACT

The Fortress contains an Imperial training dojo, prison cells, an interrogation chamber, and the tombs of fallen Jedi.

This part of the Fortress is above the water

TOP SECURITY

Although it is guarded by legions of stormtroopers and fitted with the latest Imperial technology, the Fortress can be breached. Obi-Wan Kenobi rescues a young Princess Leia from here, with a little inside help, and Jedi Cal Kestis also breaks in.

FORTRESS VADER

When Darth Vader wanted a planet of his own, he chose Mustafar. Only the toughest creatures can withstand the red-hot volcanic lava there, making it an ideal location for a Sith Lord's personal retreat.

MUSTAFAR

Darth Vader feels a strong dark side connection to Mustafar. It's the place where his old friend Obi-Wan left him for dead, before Darth Sidious rescued and rebuilt him.

It was not easy building on Mustafar— it took nine attempts

BUILDING A FORTRESS

The castle was designed by the ancient Sith Lord Darth Momin, whose spirit had been preserved in a mask. It is built on the site of an ancient Sith cave.

SHOW OF FORCE

The central tower is made from obsidian, which is thought to have dark side properties. The two tall towers at the top are also thought to channel the dark side.

SITH FACT

Vader plans to use the Sith cave beneath his fortress to create a path directly to the dark side, in order to bring his wife, Padmé, back from the dead.

VADER'S SANCTUM

Vader often goes to his fortress to rest inside a bacta tank. It's the only place he can survive without the mask and armor that keep him alive.

CAN OBJECTS CARRY THE DARK SIDE?

While the Jedi try to live simple, peaceful lives with few possessions, the Sith are the opposite. They strive for power, often using objects to help them channel the Force or to hide dark side secrets. These artifacts are dangerous and powerful, so many who oppose the dark side try to find and destroy them.

SITH HOLOCRON

Holocrons are used by the Sith and the Jedi to store information (or to hide it). A Sith holocron can even turn Force-sensitive individuals toward the dark side, as Ezra Bridger discovers. Fortunately, his master takes it away before it is too late.

SITH WAYFINDER

Shaped like Sith holocrons, wayfinders are designed to guide the Sith to mysterious areas of the galaxy such as the Unknown Regions. Made using ancient technology, only Force users can operate them.

INTERROGATION CHAIR

The Inquisitors and the First Order have used these pain-inducing chairs to extract information. However, when Kylo Ren puts Rey in the chair, she uses the Force to read his thoughts instead.

MASK OF DARTH MOMIN

Darth Momin's body was destroyed, but his consciousness remained inside his mask. Years later, Darth Sidious gives Vader the mask to help him build his fortress on Mustafar.

BRIGHT STAR

Vader wants to use this sacred artifact from Mustafar to bring back his wife, Padmé. However, he is thwarted halfway through the ritual, and the Bright Star is destroyed.

ASHAS REE POWER SOURCE

Hidden underground in a Sith temple on the planet Ashas Ree, this Sith relic is located by treasure hunter Mika Grey. She wants to stop the First Order from getting the relic, but ends up using it and draining its power.

SWORD OF KHASHYUN

Legend has it that this dark side artifact was created by ancient Sith warriors who preferred swords to lightsabers. It was last seen at Dok-Ondar's Den of Antiquities on the planet Batuu.

PALPATINE'S SITH CHALICE

While pretending to be a regular politician, Darth Sidious keeps this ancient Sith chalice on display in his chambers. No one realizes what the object is, and none question why Chancellor Palpatine would possess it.

LIGHTSABERS OF DARTH ATRIUS

Darth Atrius' ancient pair of lightsabers have the power to make anyone who wields them fall into a killing frenzy. Even Darth Vader thinks they are too dangerous. He destroys one of the lightsabers, and Luke Skywalker destroys the other.

FOURTH SISTER

DARK SIDE STATUS

- ☐ Fallen Jedi
- ☑ Inquisitor
- ☐ Acolyte
- ☐ Dark Lord
- ☐ Other

Much of Fourth Sister's past remains a mystery. Like many Inquisitors, she was a Jedi who survived Order 66 and then fell to the dark side. As an Inquisitor, she hunts any surviving Jedi, including Obi-Wan Kenobi.

Standard black uniform

KEY FACTS

Homeworld: Unknown
Species: Unknown
Height: 1.68 m (5ft 6 in)
Trained by: Darth Sidious, Darth Vader
Appearances: OWK

SITH FACT

Rebel Alliance commander Lina Graf once impersonated Fourth Sister to get access to Fortress Vader and rescue a comrade.

IMPORTANT MISSION

Fourth Sister is not as brutal as Fifth Brother or as ambitious as Third Sister, and she has no loyalty to her fellow Inquisitors. She tells the Grand Inquisitor about Third Sister's plot to send bounty hunters after Obi-Wan.

GRAND INQUISITOR

A former Jedi, the Grand Inquisitor was one of Darth Sidious' easiest recruits to the Inquisitorius. Even as a Jedi he was drawn to the dark side, and had come to despise the Jedi Order.

DARK SIDE STATUS

Fallen Jedi ☐
Inquisitor ☑
Acolyte ☐
Dark Lord ☐
Other ☐

Protective coverings for hyper-sensitive ears

SITH FACT

As a Jedi Knight, the Grand Inquisitor was a guard at the Jedi Temple. This gave him access to lots of secret information via the Jedi Archives.

KEY FACTS

Homeworld: Utapau
Species: Pau'an
Height: 1.98 m (6 ft 6 in)
Trained by: Darth Sidious, Darth Vader
Appearances: C, OWK, R

RUTHLESS MASTER

When the Grand Inquisitor first met Darth Vader, they fought a duel. Now, the Grand Inquisitor is loyal to his Sith Master and carries out his orders with ruthless efficiency.

KURUK

 DARK SIDE STATUS
- ☐ Fallen Jedi
- ☐ Inquisitor
- ☐ Acolyte
- ☐ Dark Lord
- ☑ Other

One of the Knights of Ren, Kuruk is a skilled sniper. During a battle, his job is usually to hang back and protect the other Knights with his rifle. He rarely misses.

Side panels block peripheral vision so Kuruk can focus on his target

SITH FACT

Although Kuruk is Force sensitive and follows the dark side, he has never been trained to use his abilities.

KEY FACTS

Homeworld: Unknown
Species: Humanoid
Height: 1.79 m (5ft 10 in)
Trained by: Untrained
Appearances: VII, IX, C

TAKING CHEWIE

On a mission to Pasaana for the First Order, Kuruk helps to capture Chewbacca. He delivers him, and an ancient Sith dagger, to the First Order stormtroopers.

MALACHOR

Malachor is a lifeless and barren planet in the Outer Rim, an appropriate location for a Sith temple. Thousands of years old, the temple lies far beneath the surface of the planet. As younglings, Jedi are warned never to go there.

SUPERWEAPON

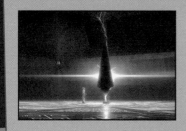

When Ezra Bridger visits Malachor, the Padawan discovers that the temple is a giant superweapon that has the power to wipe out all life. Fortunately Ezra is able to destroy the temple without firing the weapon.

SITH FACT

Centuries ago, a Jedi-Sith battle took place on Malachor. The Sith temple's weapon misfired and turned everyone on the planet to stone.

CHARACTER

⊛ DARK SIDE STATUS

- ☐ Fallen Jedi
- ☐ Inquisitor
- ☐ Acolyte
- ☐ Dark Lord
- ☑ Other

Few can match Kylo´s skill with a lightsaber

SITH FACT

Kylo Ren isn't a Sith or a Jedi. He uses his knowledge of both sides of the Force to serve the First Order.

FAMILY RESEMBLANCE

Kylo wishes that he could have met his grandfather, Darth Vader. He longs to have his strength and power, and Vader's charred helmet is his most treasured possession.

SUPREME LEADER

After killing his father, Han Solo, Kylo can see no way back from the dark side, so he sets out to rule the galaxy himself. He kills Snoke and takes over as Supreme Leader, and plans to defeat Darth Sidious, too.

FORCE DYAD

Kylo shares a special Force bond with Rey. They can communicate from opposite sides of the galaxy and feel each other's thoughts. Rey senses that there is good in Kylo, but he wants her to become his dark side apprentice.

KYLO REN

With his Force abilities, Kylo Ren, aka Ben Solo, could have been a legendary Jedi like his uncle Luke. However, fear and doubt led him to the dark side. Impatient, insecure, and destructive, Kylo is feared even by his allies.

Kylo´s mask looks intimidating and also makes his voice deeper and louder

KEY FACTS

Homeworld:	Chandrila
Species:	Human
Height:	1.89 m (6 ft 2 in)
Trained by:	Luke Skywalker, Snoke
Appearances:	VII, VIII, IX, C

WHY ARE SITH LIGHTSABERS RED?

Every Jedi makes their own lightsaber as part of their training, and each Sith constructs their own weapon, too. Both Jedi and Sith weapons have blades of energy produced by kyber crystals, but while Jedi blades can vary in color, Sith blades are always red. This is because they "bleed" their crystals by flooding them with negative emotions such as rage, hate, fear, and pain.

MAUL'S DOUBLE-BLADED LIGHTSABER

SITH FACT
The length of the blade generally varies according to the size of the user, but the style of the handle (hilt) is down to individual choice.

DARTH SIDIOUS' LIGHTSABER

Sidious' hilt is made from phrik, which is virtually indestructible.

DARTH VADER'S LIGHTSABER

Vader can make his dual-phase lightsaber blade longer or shorter in battle.

DARTH TYRANUS' LIGHTSABER

Darth Tyranus' curved hilt allows him to wield his lightsaber with one hand.

KYLO REN'S LIGHTSABER

Anyone can use a lightsaber, and a few non-Sith, such as Kylo Ren, carry red-bladed lightsabers, too.

INQUISITOR'S LIGHTSABER

The Inquisitors carry a unique double-bladed, spinning lightsaber.

MERRIN

DARK SIDE STATUS

- ☐ Fallen Jedi
- ☐ Inquisitor
- ☐ Acolyte
- ☐ Dark Lord
- ☑ Other

Merrin is a powerful foe turned hero who possesses knowledge of the Nightsisters' Force abilities (known as magick). As a child she survived a massacre of the Nightsisters ordered by Darth Tyranus. Misled to believe that the Jedi were responsible, she once hated them.

TRUSTING THE JEDI

Fallen Jedi Taron Malicos convinces Merrin that the Jedi are her enemies, but Cal Kestis shows her the truth. Merrin joins the former Jedi Padawan's crew on the *Stinger Mantis*.

Distinctive facial markings

SITH FACT

Merrin can use her magick to turn invisible, lift heavy objects without touching them, and even make her allies stronger in battle.

KEY FACTS

Homeworld:	Dathomir
Species:	Dathomirian
Height:	Unknown
Affiliation:	Nightsisters
Appearances:	JFO

MORABAND

This dusty red planet is considered to be the Sith homeworld. Like many other worlds touched by the Sith, Moraband is a desolate wasteland, with no signs of life. It is the final resting place for Darth Bane, the Sith who created the Rule of Two that the Sith live by.

FINDING ANSWERS

Grand Master Yoda finds many Sith phantasms on Moraband, all wanting to turn him to the dark side. Yoda's Force abilities are strong enough to resist, but he does not stay long on the planet.

SITH FACT

Other visitors to Moraband include Darth Sidious and Luke Skywalker. Each wants to learn more about the Force, but for very different reasons.

Below the mountains is the Valley of the Dark Lords

MOTHER TALZIN

DARK SIDE STATUS

- ☐ Fallen Jedi
- ☐ Inquisitor
- ☐ Acolyte
- ☐ Dark Lord
- ☑ Other

Mother Talzin is a powerful witch and leader of the Nightsisters. She possesses many powers connected to the dark side, including the ability to see events happening on the other side of the galaxy or even in the future.

Traditional Nightsister headdress and robes

DEFENSIVE SKILLS

When under attack, Talzin can summon a green bubble to protect her. It can absorb blaster fire and Force lightning, while still allowing her to fire her own Force lightning from inside the bubble.

KEY FACTS

Homeworld:	Dathomir
Species:	Zabrak (Dathomirian)
Height:	1.98 m (6 ft 6 in)
Affiliation:	Nightsisters
Appearances:	CW

SITH FACT

Talzin once hoped to become Sidious' apprentice, but he tricked her and kidnapped her son Maul instead.

MUSTAFAR

Mustafar was once a thriving garden world, powered by the Bright Star artifact. However, when the artifact was stolen, Mustafar became a fiery, volcanic planet with strong links to the dark side. Crime flourished there, and Darth Vader felt a strong connection to the planet.

BEFORE VADER

During the Clone Wars, Anakin Skywalker was a brave Jedi. Along with his Padawan, Ahsoka Tano, he rescued some Force-sensitive children who had been taken to Mustafar by a bounty hunter.

SITH FACT

When the Bright Star artifact was finally returned to Mustafar, the planet slowly started to heal and return to its former state.

Hot lava covers large parts of the planet

NIGHTBROTHERS

This powerful clan of male warriors follows the tradition of Dathomirian dark side users. The Nightbrothers are strong and fierce, but their Force abilities are usually quite limited. The clan is ruled by the far more powerful Nightsisters.

Viscus

TEAMING UP

Nightbrothers are trained to be fast, agile fighters. Few can match their strength; even the Jedi. Their Force abilities can mostly be seen in their increased agility and amazing reflexes.

SUPREME FIGHTERS

Nightbrothers don't seem to feel pain like other creatures. Some Nightbrothers, like Savage Opress, also have their strength and abilities enhanced by the Nightsisters' magick.

SITH FACT

The most Force-sensitive Nightbrothers often become Sith. Maul was kidnapped by Sidious to be his apprentice; later Savage Opress became Tyranus' apprentice.

Savage
Opress

Feral

NIGHTSISTERS

This powerful clan of Force-sensitive females uses the dark side of the Force differently to most. They use the magical ithor found on Dathomir to practice what they call "magick." The Nightsisters use Force spells to create illusions and to manipulate others into doing what they want.

Karis

COMING HOME

When she is betrayed by her Sith Master Darth Tyranus, Asajj Ventress returns to the Nightsisters. Together they plot to destroy Tyranus, but their plans fail. Instead, Tyranus wipes out virtually all the Nightsisters in retaliation.

BEYOND DEATH

The Nightsisters differ to the Sith and fellow dark side users in other ways, too. They are not driven by a thirst for power or desire for immortality, but simply to ensure their own survival—whatever that takes.

Naa'leth

Talia

SITH FACT

No one is really sure how the Nightsisters began, but one possible origin is that the clan was founded by Allya, an exiled Jedi.

53

NINTH SISTER

DARK SIDE STATUS

- ☐ Fallen Jedi
- ☑ Inquisitor
- ☐ Acolyte
- ☐ Dark Lord
- ☐ Other

Masana Tide was one of the few Jedi to survive Order 66, but in the aftermath she could not resist the dark side. Now known as Ninth Sister, she is a member of the ruthless Inquisitorius and willingly serves Emperor Palpatine.

KEY FACTS

Homeworld: Dowut
Species: Dowutin
Height: Unknown
Trained by: Unknown Jedi, Darth Vader
Appearances: JFO, C

SITH FACT

Ninth Sister lost her left eye during a training session with Darth Vader, and Sixth Brother cut off her right leg to save himself in battle.

Large, clawed fingers

USEFUL SKILL

Ninth Sister's strongest Force ability is being able to read others' thoughts. This ability increased when she turned to the dark side, and is very helpful to the Inquisitors.

OCHI OF BESTOON

Although Ochi believes that the dark side guides his actions, he has no actual Force abilities. He serves whoever he thinks is the most powerful, and has killed many Jedi as well as Rey's parents.

DARK SIDE STATUS

Fallen Jedi ☐
Inquisitor ☐
Acolyte ☑
Dark Lord ☐
Other ☐

Cybernetic implants help Ochi to see after he is blinded

KEY FACTS

Homeworld: Bestoon
Species: Humanoid
Height: 1.83 m (6 ft)
Affiliation: Sith Order, Crimson Dawn
Appearances: IX, C, N

Ochi carries a Sith dagger

SITH FACT

Ochi has a clue to the location of the Emperor's wayfinder, so Luke Skywalker pursues him. However, Ochi dies, trapped in the sinking sands on Pasaana.

VITAL CLUE

A Resistance team finds Ochi's ship and stolen droid on Pasaana. BB-8 reactivates the droid, D-O, and it's able to provide the clue they need from its memory.

WHAT VEHICLES DO SITH USE?

The Sith utilize a variety of vehicles in their quest for power and galactic domination. Some are small and stealthy, designed to travel short distances at great speed without being detected. Others are larger and packed with weapons, designed to cause instant destruction and generate maximum fear.

BLOODFIN

Darth Maul uses this modified speeder to track the Jedi on Naboo. He launches probe droids from it to spy on his enemies. When not in use, *Bloodfin* is kept on Maul's ship, *Scimitar*.

SCIMITAR

Maul's Sith Infiltrator, *Scimitar*, has also been heavily modified. It features a cloaking device, so it cannot be detected by other ships, as well as six laser cannons and a torpedo launcher. It can also track other ships through hyperspace.

NIGHT BUZZARD

The Knights of Ren's ship, *Night Buzzard,* is not only their mode of transport, but it's also their main base. A converted prison ship, its cells are mostly now living quarters. Some cells do remain though, as Chewbacca finds out.

FINAL ORDER FLEET

Each of the 1,080 ships in the Sith Eternal's Final Order fleet has an axial superlaser cannon capable of destroying an entire planet. It's the largest fleet that the galaxy has ever seen—the extra-large Star Destroyers are more than 2 km (1.2 miles) long with nearly 30,000 crew serving on each one.

EXECUTOR

At 19,000 m (62,300 ft) long, Darth Vader's flagship Super Star Destroyer, *Executor*, is bigger than most other ships in the Imperial fleet. With more than 5,000 turbolasers and ion cannons, it leads the Imperial forces against the Rebels at Hoth and Endor.

TIE SILENCER

Kylo Ren is not a Sith, but he is a skilled pilot just like his grandfather, Darth Vader. He flies this TIE space superiority fighter. Fast and heavily armed, its flight controls are customized especially for Kylo.

TIE WHISPER

Kylo Ren has two TIE interceptors specially modified to increase their speed, firepower, and range. Despite this, Rey is able to destroy one with her lightsaber and later set fire to the other.

SCYTHE

This sleek, angular starship transports the Inquisitors all over the galaxy. When it touches down on a planet, the inhabitants had better hope that no Jedi are found to be hiding there...

OLD DAKA

DARK SIDE STATUS

- ☐ Fallen Jedi
- ☐ Inquisitor
- ☐ Acolyte
- ☐ Dark Lord
- ☑ Other

Daka is the oldest and wisest of the Nightsisters, and often shares her knowledge with the rest of the clan. However, there are some spells that only Daka can perform, such as raising the spirits of dead Nightsisters.

KEY FACTS

Homeworld: Dathomir
Species: Zabrak (Dathomirian)
Height: 1.83 m (6 ft)
Affiliation: Nightsisters
Appearances: CW

Headdress is made of bones

SITH FACT

Daka's magicks are strong and she can see into the future. However, age has left her physical body weak and vulnerable.

WITCH'S ORB

When Count Dooku orders General Grievous and his army to destroy the Nightsisters, Old Daka uses her witch's orb to summon dead Nightsisters to help them in battle.

REN

Every leader of the Knights of Ren is known as "Ren." However, very little is known about this Ren. Although he is loyal to the dark side, he can be friendly and engaging when trying to recruit others such as Ben Solo.

DARK SIDE STATUS

Fallen Jedi ☐
Inquisitor ☐
Acolyte ☐
Dark Lord ☐
Other ☑

DARK SIDE SCARS

As many others have found, the dark side leaves its mark. Ren displays his scarred and burned body with pride, and searches the galaxy for others to join his cause.

SITH FACT

It is thought that Ren killed his predecessor and took his lightsaber. Unfortunately for Ren, he will lose his position in the same way.

Tattered cloak

KEY FACTS

Homeworld: Unknown
Species: Human
Height: Unknown
Affiliation: Knights of Ren
Appearances: C

SAVAGE OPRESS

DARK SIDE STATUS

- ☐ Fallen Jedi
- ☐ Inquisitor
- ☐ Acolyte
- ☐ Dark Lord
- ☑ Other

Savage Opress was a regular Nightbrother until his mother, Talzin, used her magick to transform him into a mighty warrior. Bigger, stronger, and with a greater connection to the Force, Savage is a fearsome opponent.

Double-bladed lightsaber

Zabrak horns

KEY FACTS

Homeworld: Dathomir
Species: Zabrak (Dathomirian)
Height: 2.18 m (7 ft 2 in)
Trained by: Viscus, Asajj Ventress, Darth Tyranus, Darth Maul
Appearances: CW, C

SITH FACT

The Nightsisters send Savage to serve Tyranus because they secretly want him to assassinate the Sith Lord. At first, Savage does not know about their plan.

SITH TRAINING

Savage is a master of lightsaber combat, thanks to training from Tyranus and later his brother, Maul. Savage can fight several Jedi at once, with ease.

SECOND SISTER

The Inquisitor known as Second Sister is a former Jedi, Trilla Suduri. She was once compassionate and kind, but she is now driven by hatred and cruelty, especially toward the Jedi.

DARK SIDE STATUS

Fallen Jedi ☐
Inquisitor ☑
Acolyte ☐
Dark Lord ☐
Other ☐

Helmet makes Second Sister look intimidating

FEARED MASTER

Although she is a cunning and ruthless Inquisitor, there is one thing that Second Sister fears—her master, Darth Vader. She knows that if she fails in a mission, Vader will punish her.

SITH FACT

Trilla Suduri's Jedi Master, Cere Junda, was forced into revealing her Padawan's location. Feeling betrayed, Trilla gave in to the dark side.

KEY FACTS

Homeworld: Unknown
Species: Human
Height: Unknown
Trained by: Cere Junda, Darth Vader
Appearances: JFO

61

SEVENTH SISTER

DARK SIDE STATUS

- ☐ Fallen Jedi
- ☑ Inquisitor
- ☐ Acolyte
- ☐ Dark Lord
- ☐ Other

Unlike many Inquisitors, Seventh Sister doesn't always kill her enemies. She is an agile and skilled fighter, but likes to tease and verbally spar with her opponents, too.

Seventh sister can scratch her foes using the Force

SITH FACT

Seventh Sister is a former Jedi. She escaped Order 66, but fell to the dark side soon after. Now she hunts Jedi.

KEY FACTS

Homeworld: Mirial
Species: Mirialan
Height: 1.79 m (5 ft 10in)
Trained by: Yoda, Darth Sidious
Appearances: R

COMRADES

Seventh Sister regularly teams up with Fifth Brother. Their different sizes and fighting styles make them a formidable team, although they sometimes disagree about the best strategy.

SITH CITADEL

This ancient Sith fortress on Exegol is thousands of years old, and can only be found with the help of a special wayfinder. It is here that Darth Sidious hides as he cheats death and where, once fully restored, he plans to transform the galaxy into a Sith empire once more.

DARK THRONE

The imposing Sith throne is located in the center of the Sith Citadel. Sidious is confident that it will be the seat of his newly restored power, but Rey, his granddaughter, disagrees.

SITH FACT

Luke Skywalker spent years looking for a wayfinder to Exegol. Kylo Ren finds one at Fortress Vader and Rey finds the other in the ruins of the second Death Star.

SITH ETERNAL

Every Sith is dedicated to the dark side, but the Sith Eternal take devotion to a whole new level. The members of this secretive cult have all sworn to do whatever it takes to help Darth Sidious take his rightful place—as Sith ruler of the galaxy.

EXPERIMENTS

Darth Sidious prepared for his inevitable death by having the Sith Eternal develop cloning technology. This also enabled them to create artificial life-forms with Sith powers, known as strandcasts.

SITH FACT

The Sith Eternal have spent years preparing to take over the galaxy, including constructing the Final Order fleet of Star Destroyers.

SIXTH BROTHER

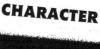

As Jedi Bil Valen, Sixth Brother was trained to help others and to act with compassion. However, as an Inquisitor Sixth Brother's mission is to search the galaxy looking for any surviving Jedi, and then to eliminate them.

DARK SIDE STATUS

- Fallen Jedi ☐
- Inquisitor ☑
- Acolyte ☐
- Dark Lord ☐
- Other ☐

Blue helmet is usually worn covering face

SITH FACT

Sixth brother has a cybernetic arm. Vader cut the original off in a training session in order to teach him about loss.

Spinning lightsaber can also be thrown like a boomerang

KEY FACTS

Homeworld: Unknown
Species: Unknown
Height: Unknown
Trained by: Darth Vader
Appearances: N, C

WHATEVER IT TAKES

Sixth Brother doesn't care about anyone else. When some purge troopers are tricked into turning on the Inquisitors, he cuts Ninth Sister's leg off so that he can escape.

⚙ DARK SIDE STATUS

- ☐ Fallen Jedi
- ☐ Inquisitor
- ☐ Acolyte
- ☐ Dark Lord
- ☑ Other

SITH FACT

Snoke once fought Luke Skywalker. The Jedi was the cause of some of the scars on Snoke's body.

⚡ CREATING FEAR

Fear is one of the dark side's greatest weapons. Snoke remains a shadowy figure, and is rarely seen in person. He gives orders via hologram, projecting his image at a monstrous size.

✗ SNOKE'S MISTAKE

Snoke doesn't believe Rey when she senses that there is still good in Kylo Ren. He commands Kylo to kill Rey, but Kylo refuses. Instead, he strikes down his master and takes Snoke's place as Supreme Leader.

ORIGINS REVEALED

After Snoke's death Kylo learns that his master was a genetic strandcast (clone) created by Darth Sidious. Snoke had no idea that he was merely a puppet, doing exactly what Sidious wanted.

SNOKE

The Supreme Leader of the First Order is a mysterious and terrifying dictator. Snoke believes that he is the most powerful Force user in the galaxy, and utilizes the Force to rule through fear and cruelty. But even Snoke doesn't know his true origins.

Battle scars

Golden Khalat robes

KEY FACTS

Homeworld:	Exegol
Species:	Genetic strandcast
Height:	2.1 m (6 ft 11 in)
Trained by:	Darth Sidious
Apprentice:	Kylo Ren
Appearances:	VII, VIII, IX, C

TARON MALICOS

DARK SIDE STATUS

- ☑ Fallen Jedi
- ☐ Inquisitor
- ☐ Acolyte
- ☐ Dark Lord
- ☐ Other

Jedi Taron Malicos escaped Order 66 but became stranded on Dathomir. There, he turned to the dark side, unable to resist the planet's connection to the Force. Now he craves power, and is leader of the Nightbrothers.

TELLING LIES

Malicos lies to the Nightsister Merrin, telling her that the Jedi killed her family. He wants her to trust him so that she will teach him how to use dark side Force magick.

SITH FACT

Malicos takes control of the Nightbrothers by killing Viscus. He does not tell anyone that he was once a Jedi Master.

Scars from battles against Nightbrothers who opposed him

KEY FACTS

Homeworld:	Unknown
Species:	Human
Height:	Unknown
Affiliations:	Jedi Order, Nightbrothers
Appearances:	JFO

TENTH BROTHER

Although Tenth Brother cannot see, he is highly skilled with a lightsaber. His exceptional hearing and Force abilities make him a formidable foe. However, his tendency to be over-confident may be his downfall.

DARK SIDE STATUS

Fallen Jedi ☐
Inquisitor ☑
Acolyte ☐
Dark Lord ☐
Other ☐

SITH FACT

Tenth Brother was once a wise and respected Jedi named Prosset Dibs, but he lost faith in the Order and tried to kill Mace Windu.

KEY FACTS

Homeworld: Unknown
Species: Miraluka
Height: Unknown
Trained by: Unknown
Appearances: C

Tenth Brother wears little armor

STANDING OUT

Unlike most Inquisitors, who favor a spinning double-blade, Tenth Brother carries two lightsabers. These shoto blades are shorter than most, too.

69

TWO VS. ONE

Darth Maul faces two Jedi. He defeats Qui-Gon Jinn and appears to have beaten Obi-Wan Kenobi. However, the Jedi uses all his Force abilities to recover and seemingly kill Maul.

RETREAT

Although the Sith want to win at all costs, sometimes it is not possible. Darth Tyranus cannot defeat Yoda, so he distracts the Jedi and escapes.

SITH VS. JEDI

YODA VS. SIDIOUS

Even the mighty Grand Master Yoda cannot defeat Darth Sidious. However, the wise Jedi senses that although he might not win this duel, all is not lost for the Jedi.

FRIEND TO FOE

Obi-Wan Kenobi trained Anakin Skywalker, but later they meet as enemies. On Mustafar Obi-Wan is the victor, but on Mapuzo Darth Vader proves stronger.

FINAL DUEL

When Vader and Obi-Wan duel for a fourth and final time, Obi-Wan ends the battle by becoming one with the Force. Only his Jedi cloak and lightsaber are left behind.

With a power-hungry enemy like the Sith, conflict is inevitable. Over the centuries, the Sith and Jedi have fought many times, from the epic Jedi-Sith Wars to many closely fought duels. Although a Sith will stop at nothing to win, the light side gives the Jedi great strength and courage.

FATHER VS. SON

The first time Darth Vader fights Luke Skywalker, the Sith cuts off the young Jedi's hand and asks him to join the dark side. When Luke refuses, Vader reveals that he is Luke's father.

SITH FACT

It's never too late to turn back to the light side. When Darth Sidious urges his apprentice to kill Luke Skywalker, Vader kills his master instead.

THE SON

DARK SIDE STATUS

- [ ] Fallen Jedi
- [ ] Inquisitor
- [ ] Acolyte
- [ ] Dark Lord
- [x] Other

The Son comes from a family of beings known as "Force-wielders." His sister, the Daughter, follows the light side, but he has chosen the dark side. The Father tries to keep balance between the two sides.

The Son can also transform into a much larger gargoyle form

SITH FACT

The Son and his family live in the mysterious realm known as Mortis, where some believe the Force itself originates.

KEY FACTS

Homeworld: Mortis
Species: Force-wielder
Height: 2.2 m (7 ft 2 in)
Affiliation: Force-wielders
Appearances: CW

DARK SIDE PLOT

The Son plots to lure Anakin Skywalker to the dark side. He sends a distress signal that brings the Jedi to Mortis, along with Obi-Wan and Ahsoka. He does not succeed in corrupting Anakin... this time.

THIRD SISTER

Ruthless and ambitious, Third Sister is totally focused on completing her mission. If she succeeds in capturing Obi-Wan Kenobi, she knows that it will please Darth Vader. She hopes to be made Grand Inquisitor, but only so she can then betray Vader.

DARK SIDE STATUS
Fallen Jedi ☐
Inquisitor ☑
Acolyte ☐
Dark Lord ☐
Other ☐

KEY FACTS

Homeworld: Unknown
Species: Human
Height: 1.7 m (5 ft 7 in)
Trained by: Yoda, Darth Vader
Appearances: OWK

Third Sister wears a billowing cape

SITH FACT

Third Sister is the former Jedi youngling Reva Sevander. She is secretly plotting revenge on the person who killed her fellow Jedi younglings— Darth Vader.

SMART SISTER

Third Sister is athletic and agile, with exceptional Force abilities. However, perhaps her greatest weapon is her mind. She sets a trap for Obi-Wan Kenobi and then tracks him across the galaxy.

TRUDGEN

DARK SIDE STATUS

- ☐ Fallen Jedi
- ☐ Inquisitor
- ☐ Acolyte
- ☐ Dark Lord
- ☑ Other

Although he has some Force abilities, Trudgen usually relies on his vibrocleaver weapon in battle. The vibrating blade has awesome cutting power, and even a lightsaber would find it tough to slice through.

Battered and patched-up helmet

Mighty vibrocleaver

NEW LEADER

When Kylo Ren becomes leader of the Knights of Ren, Trudgen and his fellow Knights follow him without hesitation. As long as he follows the dark side, they'll do as he says.

KEY FACTS

Homeworld:	Unknown
Species:	Humanoid
Height:	1.75 m (5 ft 9 in)
Affiliation:	Knights of Ren
Appearances:	VII, IX, C

SITH FACT

Trudgen's helmet originally belonged to a death trooper he defeated, but has been modified over the years.

USHAR

Ushar's weapon of choice is a war club. The end of the club contains a powerful charge, and when he strikes someone with it they rarely get up. Ushar's Force abilities are limited and untrained.

DARK SIDE STATUS

Fallen Jedi ☐
Inquisitor ☐
Acolyte ☐
Dark Lord ☐
Other ☑

SITH FACT

Ushar's helmet has breathing tubes, so it is likely that he acquired it from a non-human. Its battered appearance is due to his many battles.

End of the club contains kinetite charge

KEY FACTS

Homeworld: Unknown
Species: Humanoid
Height: 1.78 m (5 ft 10 in)
Affiliation: Knights of Ren
Appearances: VII, IX, C

WRONG SIDE

When Kylo Ren returns to the light side of the Force, the Knights of Ren attack their former master. Ushar's battle skills are no match for the highly trained Ben Solo.

75

VICRUL

DARK SIDE STATUS

- ☐ Fallen Jedi
- ☐ Inquisitor
- ☐ Acolyte
- ☐ Dark Lord
- ☑ Other

Like all the Knights of Ren, Vicrul has Force abilities but has never been trained to use them. He cannot control his abilities and they can occur spontaneously to help (or hinder) him in battle.

SITH FACT

Vicrul has enough knowledge of the Force to be able to increase his foes' feelings of fear and to enhance his reflexes in battle.

MIGHTY WEAPON

Vicrul's first-choice weapon is a lethally sharp scythe made of the virtually indestructible metal phrik. He also carries a blaster for close combat.

Coat made from the skin of a large reptilian he killed

KEY FACTS

Homeworld:	Unknown
Species:	Human
Height:	1.79 m (5 ft 10 in)
Affiliation:	Knights of Ren
Appearances:	VII, IX, C

VISCUS

Viscus is the respected leader of the Nightbrothers. A powerful warrior, he is also a clever battle strategist. Like all Nightbrothers, he has sworn to do whatever he can to serve the Nightsisters.

DARK SIDE STATUS

Fallen Jedi ☐
Inquisitor ☐
Acolyte ☐
Dark Lord ☐
Other ☑

COMMON FOE

The Jedi Anakin Skywalker and Obi-Wan Kenobi go to Dathomir to find out more about Savage Opress. Viscus is no friend of the Jedi, but he hates the Sith more and does not harm them.

KEY FACTS

Homeworld: Dathomir
Species: Zabrak (Dathomirian)
Height: 1.88 m (6 ft 2 in)
Affiliation: Nightbrothers
Appearances: CW, C

Face tattoos show his status and experience

SITH FACT

When Taron Malicos arrives on Dathomir, Viscus instinctively does not trust him. Viscus decides to kill him, but Malicos defeats him.

GLOSSARY

AGILITY
Being able to move quickly and easily.

APPRENTICE
A person who is learning a skill from an expert.

ARTIFACTS
Important or interesting objects from the past.

ASSASSIN
Someone who kills others for money.

BACTA TANK
A tank filled with bacta, a special liquid that heals injuries faster.

BESKAR
A nearly indestructible steel that Mandalorians use for armor.

BOUNTY HUNTER
Someone who tracks down and captures others for a reward (bounty).

CLAN
A large family group that includes distant relatives.

CLONE
An exact copy of another person.

CLONE WARS
A series of galaxy-wide battles between the Republic and the Separatists.

CULT
A group whose members follow an unusual religion or set of beliefs with extreme devotion.

DARK SIDE
The part of the Force associated with fear, revenge, and power.

DROID
A kind of robot.

DUEL
A fight between two people.

EMPIRE
A period when the galaxy is controlled by a single person, Emperor Palpatine. This Empire is ruled with fear and oppression.

FIRST ORDER
A military-style group led by Supreme Leader Snoke that rules the galaxy in a similar way to the Empire.

FORCE
A natural and powerful energy that flows through all living things.

GALAXY
A group of millions of stars and planets.

IMMORTALITY
Living forever.

IMPULSIVE
Acting without thinking first.

INQUISITORIUS
A group of Force-sensitive dark side agents who track down Jedi for Emperor Palpatine.

JEDI
A group that defends peace and justice in the galaxy.

KYBER CRYSTAL
A crystal that channels energy and can be used to power a lightsaber.

LIGHTSABER
A Sith or Jedi's sword-like weapon with a blade of glowing energy.

LIGHT SIDE
The part of the Force associated with peace, compassion, and healing.

MAGICK
The special abilities that the Nightsisters of Dathomir gain from the dark side of the Force.

MANIPULATE
To control or influence someone.

OBSIDIAN
A dark, glass-like rock produced by volcanoes.

ORDER 66
A secret order that made the Clone Troopers try to kill all Jedi and follow Emperor Palpatine.

PADAWAN
A Jedi apprentice.

REBELS
A collection of groups seeking to overthrow the Empire and restore the Republic.

RELIC
An object from the past.

REPUBLIC
Government of the galaxy by the people and their chosen (elected) representatives.

RESISTANCE
A group of people who want to defeat the First Order.

REVENGE
Seeking to harm someone as payback for a wrong they have done.

RITUAL
A set of actions that are always performed in the same way for an important reason.

SENATOR
An elected representative of the government (Senate).

SITH
Enemies of the Jedi who use the dark side of the Force.

SUPERWEAPON
A large and extremely powerful weapon.

VISIONS
Images that seem real but are not. They might be dreams or things that could happen in the future.

YOUNGLING
A Force-sensitive child who begins their Jedi training at the Jedi Temple.

Senior Editor David Fentiman
Senior Designer Nathan Martin
Production Editor Marc Staples
Senior Production Controller Mary Slater
Managing Editor Emma Grange
Managing Art Editor Vicky Short
Publishing Director Mark Searle

For Lucasfilm
Senior Editor Brett Rector
Editor Jennifer Pooley
Creative Director Michael Siglain
Art Director Troy Alders
Story Group Leland Chee and Kate Izquierdo
Creative Art Manager Phil Szostak
Asset Management Elinor De La Torre and Sarah Williams
Special thanks to Scott Leong, Anthony Rodriguez,
and Angela Perez de Tagle

Designed for DK by Thelma-Jane Robb

First American Edition, 2023
Published in the United States by DK Publishing
1745 Broadway, 20th Floor, New York NY 10019

DK, a Division of Penguin Random House LLC
23 24 25 26 27 10 9 8 7 6 5 4 3 2
003–333559–Apr/2023

© & TM 2023 LUCASFILM LTD

Page design copyright © 2023 Dorling Kindersley Limited

A catalog record for this book is available from
the Library of Congress.

ISBN 978-0-7440-7068-2

DK books are available at special discounts when purchased
in bulk for sales promotions, premiums, fund-raising,
or educational use. For details, contact: DK Publishing
Special Markets, 1745 Broadway, 20th Floor, New York NY 10019
SpecialSales@dk.com

Printed in China

For the curious

www.dk.com
www.starwars.com

MIX
Paper | Supporting
responsible forestry
FSC™ C018179

This book is made from
Forest Stewardship Council™
certified paper—one small
step in DK's commitment
to a sustainable future.